Say Please Amanda Louise

Nurturing Manners and Positive Behavior

Always say, Please, Thank you!

FERNE PRESS

Written by Whitney Pytlowany & Illustrated by Jeff Covieo

Say Please, Amanda Louise
Nurturing Manners and Positive Behavior

Layout and cover design by Jacqueline L. Challiss Hill
Illustrations created by Jeff Covieo
Illustrations created with digital graphics
Printed in the United States of America

Summary: Amanda Louise needs some help learning manners.

Library of Congress Cataloging-in-Publication Data
Pytlowany, Whitney
Say Please, Amanda Louise/Whitney Pytlowany–First Edition
ISBN-13: 978-1-938326-45-5
I. Manners. 2. Preschool. 3. Juvenile Fiction.
I. Pytlowany, Whitney II. Title
Library of Congress Control Number: 2015958227

FERNE PRESS

Ferne Press is an imprint of Nelson Publishing & Marketing
366 Welch Road, Northville, MI 48167
www.nelsonpublishingandmarketing.com
(248) 735-0418

For my husband, daughter, and son, thank you for the encouragement.

Amanda burped loudly
while drinking her juice.
She kept right on eating
without an excuse.

The students around her
acted pretty amazed.
"This is not behavior
our teacher would praise."

"You should say 'pardon',"
a boy turned to say.
"Maybe 'excuse me'
or 'sorry' is okay."

"We all can be rude;
it's a matter of fact.
But using our manners
is how we should act."

She talked to her friend,
the hamster named Blue,
and asked him if he
had to use manners, too.

As Blue nibbled on treats,
Amanda thought and thought.
She thought of the things
that she had been taught.

It was time for the class
to go out to play.
Amanda rushed forward
to be first that day.

She ran past the others
with a jiggle and jump.
She slipped on the rug
and hit the chair with a bump.

"Uh-oh," said Miss Emma.
"Please use walking feet.
Be slow like a turtle.
You don't have to compete."

Amanda took her place
in the middle of the line
as the class went outside
to have playtime.

She wondered out loud,
"Do you have to walk slow?
Or let others go first?
I just have to know."

As the squirrel chattered on,
Amanda thought and thought.
She thought of the things
that she had been taught.

Miss Emma called everyone
together to say,
"We have new toys
to play with today!"

Amanda was excited.
She just couldn't wait
to play with the toys
because they looked great!

She reached out to grab them
before anyone could.
But the other kids said,
"Taking turns would be good."

Amanda sat down
while Miss Emma discussed
how to take turns
without any fuss.

She wondered out loud
if he had lessons to learn.
"It's just so hard
to wait for my turn."

As Bubbles swam 'round,
Amanda thought and thought.
She thought of the things
that she had been taught.

Amanda was wondering
how it would be
to think about others
instead of just "me."

She needed some help
from a person who knew
all about manners
and what kids should do.

She thought that Miss Casey
could explain to her why
using her manners
was something to try.

So very bravely Amanda
tapped on Miss Casey's knee
and asked with a smile,
"Will you please help me?"

"Maybe each day
you can try something new.
Because changing yourself
can be hard to do."

"Choose one thing a day
and make it a plan.
Take turns or walk slow;
I know that you can!"

"You can be proud of yourself
and the work that you do.
I know you'll be happy
with these new changes, too."

While she was listening,
Amanda thought and thought.
She thought of the things
that she had been taught.

She decided to start
by walking in line.
She let others go first
and it made her feel fine.

She raised her hand
to share with the group
and said "excuse me" to friends
while she was eating her soup.

Then she waited her turn
to play with new toys
while she skipped with the girls
and jumped with the boys.

Amanda felt happy
with the praise that she earned,
but each day was tricky
to use what she learned.

Amanda was busy
with going to school.
It was hard to remember
every new rule.

But she tried very hard
to think all the time
instead of just doing
what first came to mind.

She gave up her seat
and handed over her chair
when a new girl arrived—
it seemed only fair!

They talked about school
and every class pet.
Amanda was happy
with the new friend she'd met.

While the new girl was reading
with Amanda one day,
she sneezed very loudly
but had nothing to say.

Amanda leaned over
to show her new friend
how to cover her mouth
to help the sneeze end.

AH-CHOOO!

Amanda was kind
and wanted to share
all that she knew,
to show that she cared.

So with a big smile,
she looked over and said,
"Please cover your mouth
or use your elbow instead."

"I know that it's hard
because I'm trying, too.
There are so many rules
about what you should do."

"You have to remember
to wait for your turn
and cover your mouth.
There's so much to learn!"

"My friends had to help me,
and I know they'll help you.
Because learning together
is what we all do."

Amanda's new friend
looked up as she smiled
and said, "Thank you, Amanda.
My sneezes were wild!"

Amanda felt happy
and really giggly inside.
She was learning so much
and it filled her with pride.

And now it was clear
to Amanda Louise
that it was easy to say
"thank you" and "please."

Amanda looked at her class
and she thought and thought.
She thought of the things
that she had been taught.

Amanda knew helping
her classmates was good.
So she took a deep breath
and on her tiptoes she stood.

She said to her class
with a big, silly smile,
"I'm learning new manners
and it may take me a while."

"But all of your help
is great, and it's true
that I couldn't have done it
without all of you."

"I want to say 'thank you' for helping me out because learning from friends is what school's all about."

The whole classroom cheered for Amanda Louise because they had helped her say "thank you" and "please."

Five Easy Tips for Raising a Mannerly Child

- Use your manners! Children imitate everything you do. Make your manners something they copy.

- If your child forgets to say "please" or "thank you," just repeat the "please" or "thank you" as a question. Your child will naturally respond by repeating you. Soon the words will become a habit for him to use on his own.

- Make sneezing fun! Sneeze loud and proud! Cover each sneeze with your elbow and make sure everyone sees it. Your kids will think you're funny and they will enjoy imitating you.

- Help your child hold doors open for others while you're out shopping. She will receive so much positive, complimentary feedback from shoppers that it will be an instant self-confidence boost. Your child will enjoy helping others so much, you won't be able to get her to stop!

- Allow your child to call grandparents and other loved ones on the phone to say "thank you." Your child will love the independence, your family members will get a kick out of the call, and you will be able to reinforce your child's manners with a smile on your face.

It is important for parents to understand that manners are not a natural attribute that children are born with. Children will learn manners when they are modeled by parents, siblings, and other loved ones. The easiest way to teach your child manners is to use your manners all the time for even the simplest occasion. You may think that asking your child to please pick up her room or to please hang up her coat and then thanking her when the task is accomplished is excessive, but using manners on a daily basis for even the smallest reason is the surest way to raise a mannerly child.

Allowing your preschooler to order at a restaurant and then saying "please" to the server, calling a grandparent on the phone to convey appreciation for a recently received gift, or having kids print their name on a pre-written thank you card are all personally empowering experiences for a child. By giving your child room to be independent while using his or her newly gained etiquette skills, you will be happily amazed at the responsible advances your child makes. You are the most fascinating person in your child's life and he or she can't wait to be just like you!

Author

Whitney Pytlowany has been an educator, administrator, entrepreneur, and small preschool business owner for over twenty years. She received her teaching degree from The University of Michigan-Dearborn with advanced administrative studies from Eastern Michigan University. She is an active teacher who is fully immersed in improving the self-confidence and personal motivation of her students. She is also a contributing freelance writer for local network television, where her poetry has been featured. She has been happily married for twenty-five years and is the proud mother of two mannerly children who attend The University of Michigan. For more information, please visit www.theamandalouise.com.

Illustrator

Jeff Covieo has been drawing since he could hold a pencil and hasn't stopped since. He has a BFA in photography from College for Creative Studies in Michigan and works in the commercial photography field, though drawing and illustration have been his avocation for years. *Say Please, Amanda Louise* is the thirteenth book he has illustrated.